Put Beginning Readers on the Right Track with
ALL ABOARD READING™

The All Aboard Reading series is especially designed for beginning readers. Written by noted authors and illustrated in full color, these are books that children really want to read—books to excite their imagination, expand their interests, make them laugh, and support their feelings. With fiction and nonfiction stories that are high interest and curriculum-related, All Aboard Reading books offer something for every young reader. And with four different reading levels, the All Aboard Reading series lets you choose which books are most appropriate for your children and their growing abilities.

Picture Readers

Picture Readers have super-simple texts, with many nouns appearing as rebus pictures. At the end of each book are 24 flash cards—on one side is a rebus picture; on the other side is the written-out word.

Station Stop 1

Station Stop 1 books are best for children who have just begun to read. Simple words and big type make these early reading experiences more comfortable. Picture clues help children to figure out the words on the page. Lots of repetition throughout the text helps children to predict the next word or phrase—an essential step in developing word recognition.

Station Stop 2

Station Stop 2 books are written specifically for children who are reading with help. Short sentences make it easier for early readers to understand what they are reading. Simple plots and simple dialogue help children with reading comprehension.

Station Stop 3

Station Stop 3 books are perfect for children who are reading alone. With longer text and harder words, these books appeal to children who have mastered basic reading skills. More complex stories captivate children who are ready for more challenging books.

In addition to All Aboard Reading books, look for All Aboard Math Readers™ (fiction stories that teach math concepts children are learning in school) and All Aboard Science Readers™ (nonfiction books that explore the most fascinating science topics in age-appropriate language).

All Aboard for happy reading!

Library of Congress Catalog Card Number: 95-81406

ISBN 978-0-448-41306-8   M N O P Q R S T

Too Noisy!

By Sonja Lamut

Grosset & Dunlap • New York

Once there was

an old .

He lived

in an old .

"This

is too noisy,"

said the old .

The  creaked.

The  squeaked.

And the

went bang-bang.

One day the old

took his ⌒.

Off he went to see

a very wise .

"My  is too noisy,"

said the old .

"What can I do?"

The  said,

"Take this .

The  will live

with you

in your ."

The old  took

the  to his .

The  went

maa-maa.

It broke a

with its

Crash!

So the next day

the old

went back to the .

"My  is still <u>still</u>

too noisy!" he said.

So the wise

gave him a

to take to his .

The  went

moo-moo!

The  went

maa-maa!

The old

put a

over his head.

The next day the old

went back to the .

"My  is still

too noisy!" he said.

So now the wise

gave him a

to take to his .

The  went

hee-haw, hee-haw!

The  went

moo-moo!

The  went

maa-maa!

And the old  yelled,

"It is too noisy!"

The next day the

came to the  .

She said, "Open the  .

Let out the 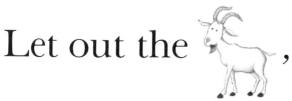 ,

the , and

the  ."

And the old  did.

And what do you know?

The  was quiet now!

The old went to

and slept all day long.

house	man
floor	door
cane	window

goat	lady
horns	chair
pillow	cow

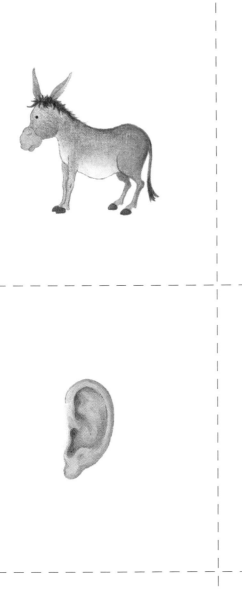

bed	donkey
dress	ear
button	brush

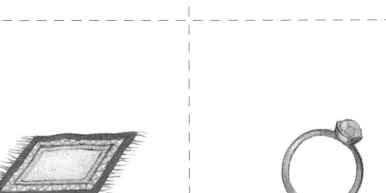

bug	hat
heart	cup
ring	rug